Ambulance in Action

Peter Bently

Illustrated by Martha Lightfoot

QED Publishing

Ambulance and its crew are in
the **ambulance station**.

Ambulance has lots of **special equipment**.
Meerkat and Ambulance Driver are checking it all.

Meerkat and Ambulance Driver jump
into Ambulance and **shut** the doors.

They put on their **seat belts.**
Ambulance Driver quickly checks the radio
for the location, and sets the satnav.

VRRROOM!

Then he turns the ignition key. Ambulance's big engine **roars** into life. They are on their way. There's **no time to lose!**

Ambulance **speeds** along the road.

Oh no, look at that traffic jam!
Ambulance Driver switches on the siren
and the warning lights.

The cars, buses and trucks hear Ambulance's siren.
They see the **flashing lights.**

Quick, move out
of the way!

NEE-NAW
NEE-NAW!

Ambulance
is coming!

Ambulance reaches the **accident**. The police
are already there and have stopped the traffic.

Meerkat grabs her
first aid bag and *leaps* out of Ambulance.

The car driver has hurt his leg.
He thinks it is broken.

Meerkat cannot get to him because the car door won't open.

Ambulance Driver radioes the controller who tells him the Fire Service are on their way.

Ambulance Driver gets the **stretcher** out of Ambulance and lowers the ramp.

He is getting everything **ready** while they wait for the Fire Service.

Meerkat stays with the car driver.

The fire crew are coming.

The fire crew use a special **cutting tool**.
Very **carefully**, they cut off the car door.

Meerkat and Ambulance Driver **lift** the car driver onto the stretcher.

Meerkat puts a **dressing** on the car driver's leg and **straps** it up.

Ambulance's crew **wheel** the stretcher into the back of Ambulance.

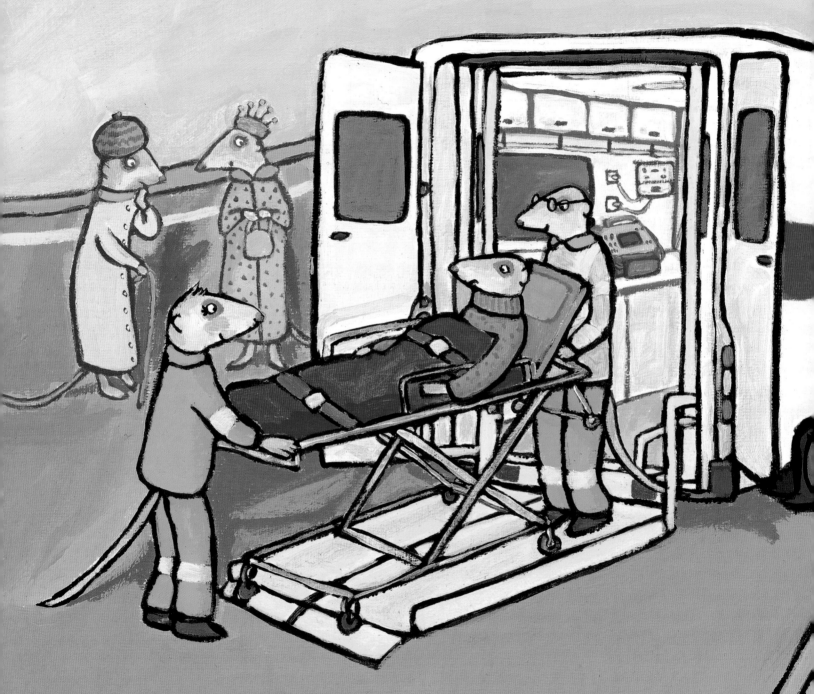

Meerkat **fixes** the stretcher in place.

Then she **raises the ramp** and **shuts** Ambulance's door.

Meerkat sits in the **back** with the car driver.

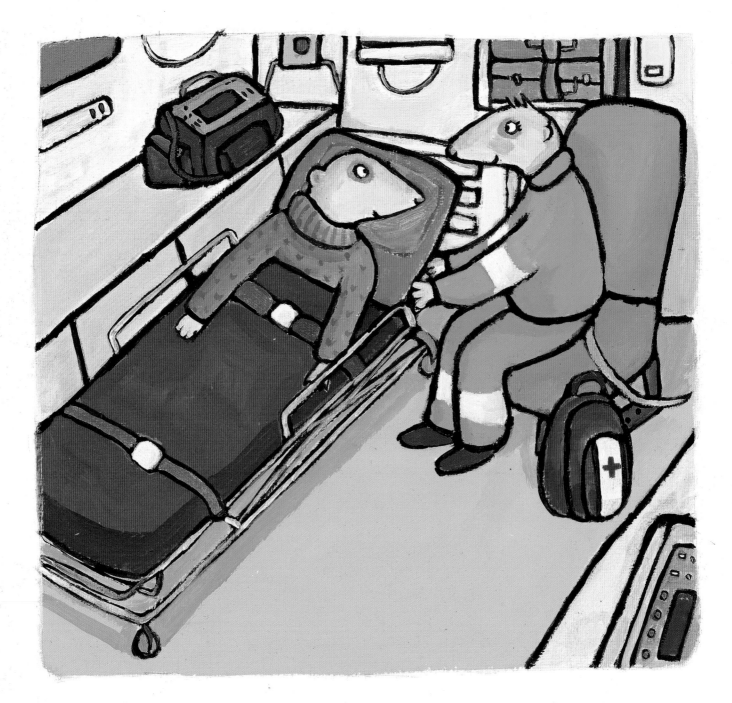

Meerkat tells him **not to worry**.
He is going to be fine.

Ambulance **speeds** off.

VRRROOM!

NEE-NAW NEE-NAW!

Ambulance Driver
radioes the hospital
so the staff there
can get ready for
their arrival.

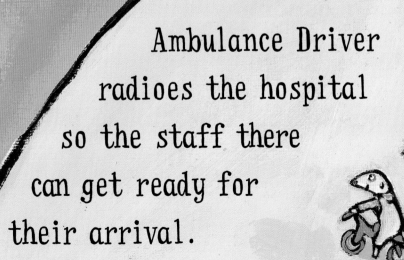

Ambulance reaches the **hospital** very quickly.
The hospital staff are waiting.

The car driver **thanks** Ambulance's crew.

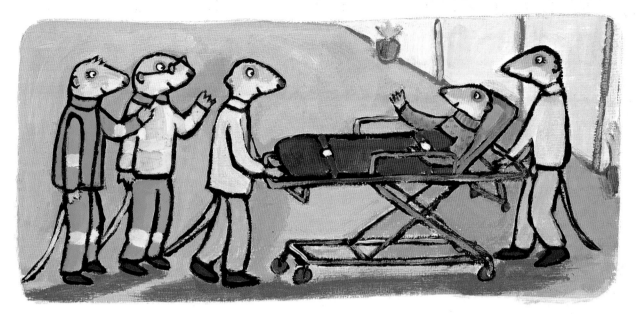

"Well done, Ambulance!" says Meerkat.
"You deserve a rest!"

Then her radio goes **beep-beep!**
"Sorry Ambulance, it's another emergency.
We must hurry!"

Let's look at
Ambulance

Wheeled stretcher/
patient bed

First aid
bag

Ramp/rear lift

Rear lights

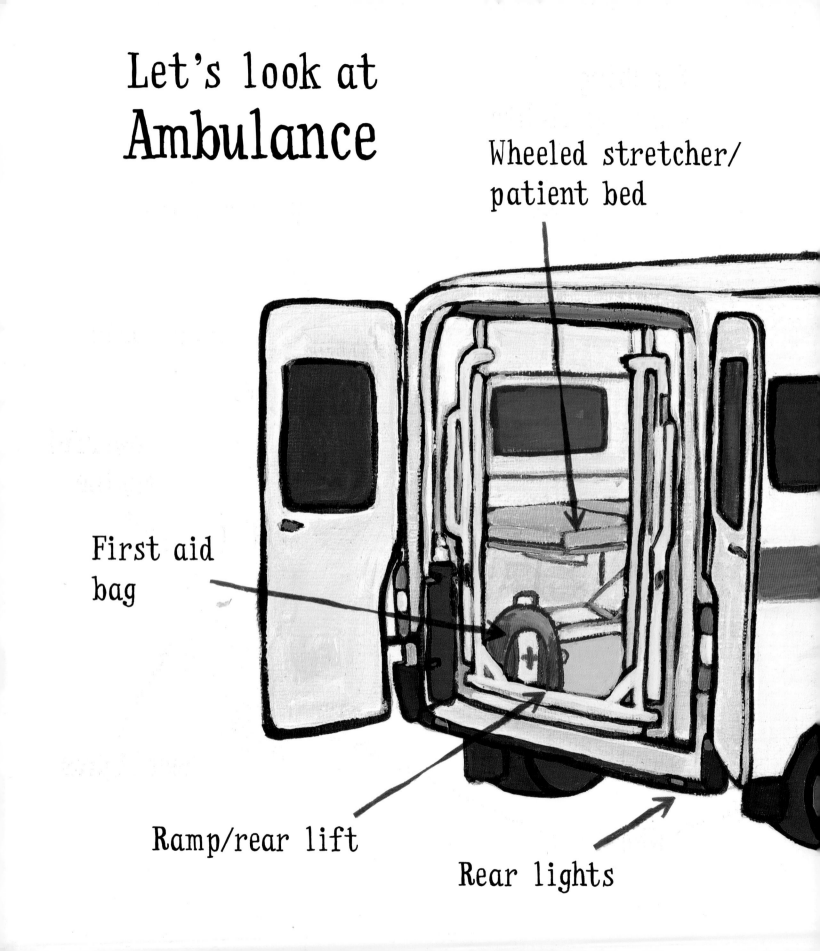

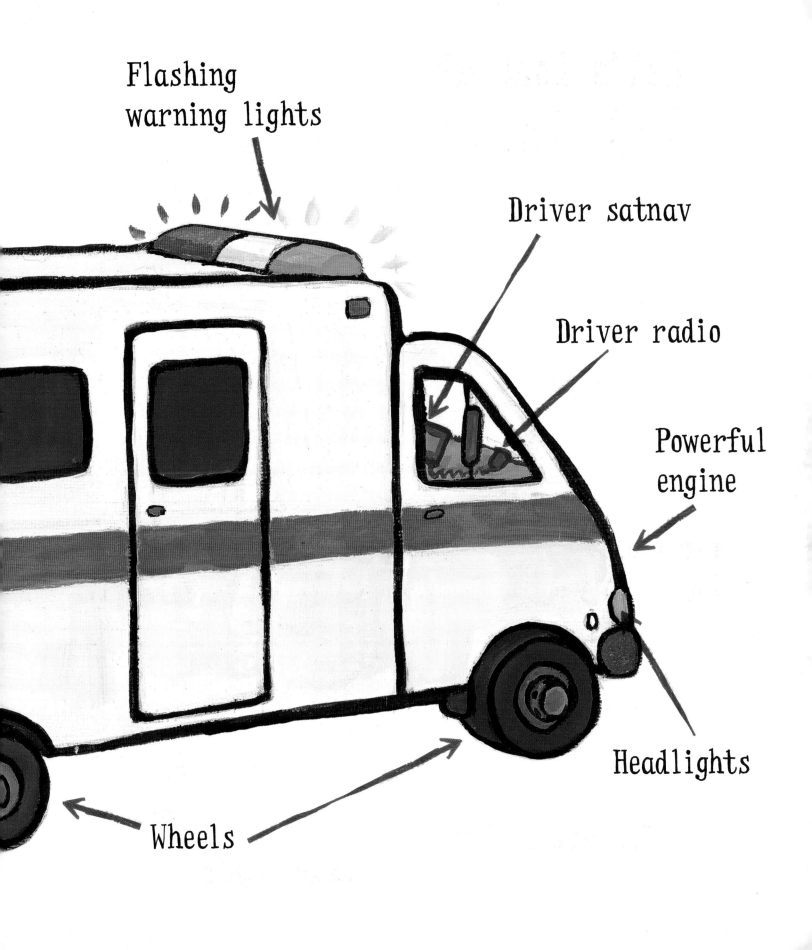

Flashing
warning lights

Driver satnav

Driver radio

Powerful
engine

Headlights

Wheels

Other Emergency Vehicles

Fire engine

Police car

Air ambulance

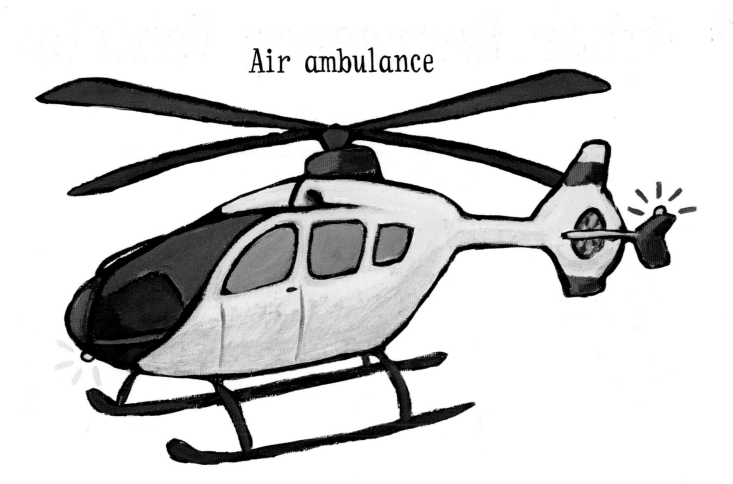

Police motorcycle

For my granny, Peggy, with thanks. M.L.
For Eli. P.B.

Designer: Plum5 Limited
Project Editor: Lucy Cuthew
Editorial Assistant: Tasha Percy

Copyright © QED Publishing 2013

First published in the UK in 2013 by
QED Publishing
A Quarto Group company
The Old Brewery, 6 Blundell Street
London, N7 9BH

www.qed-publishing.co.uk

A catalogue record for this book is available from the British Library.

ISBN: 978 1 78171 093 7

Printed in China